A MESSAGE TO PARENTS

It is of vital importance for adults to read good books to young children in order to aid their psychological and intellectual development. As well as stimulating the child's imagination. it creates a positive relationship between adult and child. Reading aloud will also help children to increase their basic vocabulary and encourage them to begin reading alone. Brown Watson has published this series of books with these aims in mind. By collecting this inexpensive library. adults and children can share hours of pleasurable reading.

Christmas
on the
Farm

Text by Maureen Spurgeon
Illustrated by Stephen Holmes

Brown Watson

ENGLAND

It was a cold, wintry afternoon at Happydale Farm.

"Soon be Christmas!" said Farmer Merry. "Time to put a Christmas tree in the hall!"

"Soon be Christmas!" said his wife. "Time to cut the holly and mistletoe. I want some nice big bunches for the dining room."

"Soon be Christmas!" cried Jenny. "Time to make cotton wool snowballs to stick on the windows."

"And make lots of paper snow-flakes!" added Peter

"Moo!" went Buttercup the cow. "Who wants cotton wool snow and paper snowflakes? You get REAL snow outside, where we are, not inside, in a house!"

"But there are LOTS of things inside!" said Lenny and Lucky, the two lambs. "Just see!"

"Maybe that's because most of Christmas happens indoors," said Denny the Donkey.

The animals talked about it for a long time. How they wished they could go indoors, just for once! "People talk about stars at Christmas," said Denny. "They're up in the sky! Look!"

As well as the stars, they saw something else.
"It's like the sledge that Jenny and Peter play with in the snow," said Denny. "A sleigh," said Hector the Horse.

"And those are reindeer!" added
Denny. "It-it's Father Christmas,
the man who brings presents on
Christmas Eve!"
"Couldn't we ask him to bring us
something?" cried Lucky.

"We don't want presents," said Hector. "We only want to go indoors to see what Christmas is like."

"Then that's what we'll wish for!" said Denny.

"What a good idea!" said the others.

But all that happened next morning was that Mrs. Merry put a sack of straw into her car. "Come along, Jenny and Peter!" she called. "Time for school!" It seemed very odd to the animals!

The straw was for the Nativity Play which told the story of the first Christmas, when Baby Jesus was born in a stable. Jenny was going to be Mary, the mother of Jesus.

Peter and his friends, Billy and Mark, were going to be the shepherds. "Baby Jesus needs a manger to lie in," said Miss Lane, their teacher. "What could we use for that?"

"We've got a REAL manger at our farm!" Peter said proudly.

"Dad would lend it to us, wouldn't he, Mum?"

"We could bring Lenny and Lucky to school, as well," said Jenny.

But the animals were disappointed
when they heard the news.
"We ALL wanted to see Christmas
indoors!" said Lucky.
"It's not fair, just me and Lenny
getting our wish."

"Tell us all about it when you get back!" said Hector.

"Don't forget anything!" squawked Hetty the Hen.

"I can LOOK indoors," said Denny, "and see for myself!"

Denny could see that Lucky and
Lenny did not like being indoors.
The children were kind and the
play was lovely. But they felt hot
and uncomfortable, and they
missed their friends.

But Miss Lane was very pleased. "You have all worked hard!" she told the children as they got ready to go home. "Look, it's beginning to snow! Just in time for Christmas, too!"

It snowed all through the night. By next morning, the snow had stopped, but it was still very, very cold. All the pipes at school had frozen. Miss West said everyone had to go home.

"No Nativity Play today!" she said. "I am sorry, children."

"Oh, dear!" said Farmer Merry. "We've brought the manger and the lambs, too." But Denny the Donkey had an idea!

He ran down the lane, braying loudly. "Hee-haw! Hee-haw!" "He wants us to go back to Happydale Farm!" said Farmer Merry. "Everyone in the school mini-bus, Miss Lane!"

Buttercup the Cow, Hector the Horse and Hetty the Hen were surprised to see Denny leading the mini-bus towards the big barn at Happydale Farm. Everyone looked so excited!

"The perfect place for our Nativity Play!" cried Miss Lane. "Change into your costumes, children!" Soon, lots of people were crowding into the barn, waiting for the play to begin.

And as well as the lambs Lenny and Lucky, Denny the Donkey, Buttercup the Cow, Hetty the Hen and Hector the Horse all appeared together in the Nativity Play.

"So THIS is what Christmas is really about!" said Denny. "I'm glad we could share in it all." "Well," said Hector the Horse, "that is what we wished for. Don't you remember?"

Not long afterwards, it was Christmas Eve. And as the reindeer pulled his magic sleigh across the sky, Father Christmas smiled down at all the animals on Happydale Farm.